Easter Egg Hunt

FIND THE HIDDEN PICTURES!

INSIGHT
KIDS

SAN RAFAEL • LOS ANGELES • LONDON

THE HUNT IS ON!

Hey there, B.B.s!

Welcome to an ultra eggs-traordinary Easter egg hunt.

Here's how you play . . .

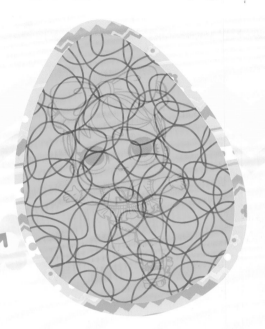

Step 1: Remove the egg-cellent spyglass from the envelope at the front of the book.

Step 2: Hold the spyglass over the mystery egg—like the one here— to reveal the object (or objects) you need to find.

Step 3: Can you identify the object in the mystery egg? It should look like this.

It's Dawn!

Step 4: Search through the scene to find Dawn. Can you find her on the opposite page?

Answers can be found in the back of the book.

(And if you ever lose the spyglass, the objects you need to search for can also be found in the back of the book.)

FLOWER UP!

BUNNY HOP 2 THE BEAT

LET'S DANCE!

BORN 2 SPARKLE

SO MANY FEELS

IN THE BAG

©MGA

SHINE BRIGHT

INSIGHT
KIDS

An Imprint of Insight Editions
PO Box 3088
San Rafael, CA 94912
www.insighteditions.com

Find us on Facebook:
www.facebook.com/InsightEditions

Follow us on Twitter:
@insighteditions

Library of Congress Cataloging-in-Publication Data available.

ISBN: 978-1-64722-239-0

Publisher: Raoul Goff
VP of Licensing and Partnerships: Vanessa Lopez
VP of Creative: Chrissy Kwasnik
VP of Manufacturing: Alix Nicholaeff
Designer: Brooke McCullum
Senior Editor: Paul Ruditis
Editorial Assistant: Elizabeth Ovieda
Managing Editor: Lauren LePera
Production Editor: Jennifer Bentham
Senior Production Manager: Greg Steffen
Senior Production Manager, Subsidiary Rights: Lina s Palma

Insight Editions, in association with Roots of Peace, will plant two trees for each tree used in the
manufacturing of this book. Roots of Peace is an internationally renowned humanitarian organization
dedicated to eradicating land mines worldwide and converting war-torn lands into productive farms
and wildlife habitats. Roots of Peace will plant two million fruit and nut trees in Afghanistan and
provide farmers there with the skills and support necessary for sustainable land use.

Manufactured in China by Insight Editions

10 9 8 7 6 5 4 3 2 1

SOME BUNNY FABULOUS

SUNNY VIBES

8

GROOVE!

U SPIN ME ROUND

ON REPEAT

TWINKLE, TWINKLE, SUPERSTARS

5

ELECTRIC DREAMS

PUMP IT UP

BLING IT UP

SHINE BRIGHT

PAJAMA PARTY!

BORN 2 SPARKLE

7

SO MANY FEELS

6

IN THE BAG

BB Boutique

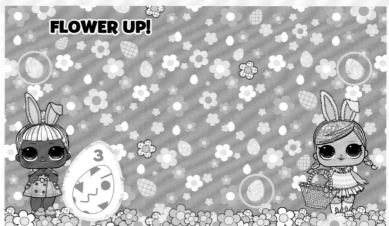

FLOWER UP!

3

BUNNY HOP 2 THE BEAT

6

LET'S DANCE!

5

SUNNY VIBES

SOME BUNNY FABULOUS

I SPY SPRINGTIME

SHAMROCK ON!

PUMP IT UP

ELECTRIC DREAMS

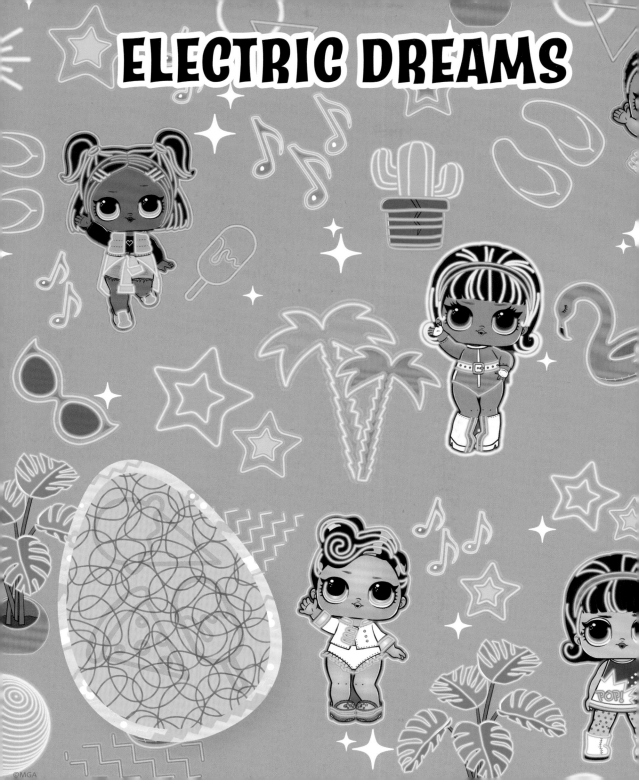